소망

아시아에서는 《바이링궐 에디션 한국 대표 소설》을 기획하여 한국의 우수한 문학을 주제별로 엄선해 국내외 독자들에게 소개합니다. 이 기획은 국내외 우수한 번역가들이 참여하여 원작의 품격을 최대한 살렸습니다. 문학을 통해 아시아의 정체성과 가치를 살피는 데 주력해 온 아시아는 한국인의 삶을 넓고 깊게 이해하는 데 이 기획이 기여하기를 기대합니다.

Asia Publishers presents some of the very best modern Korean literature to readers worldwide through its new Korean literature series 〈Bilingual Edition Modern Korean Literature〉. We are proud and happy to offer it in the most authoritative translation by renowned translators of Korean literature. We hope that this series helps to build solid bridges between citizens of the world and Koreans through a rich in-depth understanding of Korea.

바이링궐 에디션 한국 대표 소설 **101**

Bi-lingual Edition Modern Korean Literature 101

Juvesenility

채만식

소망

Ch'ae Man-Sik

ASIA
PUBLISHERS

Contents

소망

Juvesenility

남아여든 모름지기 말복날 동복을 떨쳐 입고서 종로 네거리 한복판에 가 버티고 서서 볼지니…… 외상진 싸전가게 앞을 활보해 볼지니…….

아이, 저녁이구 뭣이구 하두 맘이 뒤숭숭해서 밥 생각도 없구…….

괜찮아요, 시방 더위 같은 건 약관걸.

응. 글쎄, 그 애 아버지 말이우…… 대체 어떡허면 좋아! 생각허면 고만.

냉면? 싫어, 나는 아직 아무것두 먹구 싶잖어. 그만두구서 뭣 과일즙이나 시원하게 한 대접 타주. 언니는 저

A grown man should be able, if he wants, to plant him-self smack dab in the middle of Chongno, dressed in his winter suit in the dog days of summer, then march right past the grain shop that's got him on credit....

"*Ai*, I'm so stirred up, dinner's the last thing on my mind."

"No, it's not the heat, that's the least of my wor-ries."

"It's that husband of mine, whatever am I going to do? It absolutely irks me thinking about him."

"Cold noodles? No, like I said, I'm not in the mood for anything. On second thought, how about some

녁 잠섰수? 이 집 저녁 허구는 꽤 일렀구려.

아저씨는 왕진 나가셨나 보지? 인력거가 없구, 들어오면서 들여다보니깐 진찰실에도 안 기실 제는……

옳아, 영락없어. 그 아저씨가 진찰실에두 왕진두 안나가시구서, 언니허구 마주 안 붙어 앉었을 때가 있다가는 큰일나라구?

원 눈두 삐뚤어졌지. 우리 언니 저 아씨가 어디가 이쁜 디가 있다구 그래! 시골뜨기는 헐 수 없어. 아따 저누구냐 '쇠알?' 읽은 지가 하두 오래되서 다 잊었네, 뭣이냐《보바리 부인》남편 말이야……

허는 소리 좀 봐요. 늙어가는 동생더러 망할 년이 뭐야? 하하하. 내가 웃기는 웃는다마는, 남의 정신이지 내정신은 하나두 아니야.

양복장 새루 맞췄다더니, 벌써 들여왔구려. 아담스럽게 이쁘우. 제엔장! 나는 더러 와서 언니네가 모두 이렇게 재미나게 사는 걸 본다 치면, 새앰이 나구 속이 상해죽겠어.

무얼? 양복장을 하나 사주겠다구? 언니두 참! 누가 그까짓 양복장 말이우? 그런 건 백날 없어두 좋아. 낡으나따나 한 개 있으면 그만이지 뭐. 가난해서 좀 고생허구

fruit juice—and you have ice, right? So you already ate, Sister? Isn't it kind of early?"

"I guess Brother-in-Law's out on a house call? I didn't see his rickshaw outside, and he wasn't in the clinic either..."

"See, I'm right, process of elimination. If he's not in his office, and he's not glued to your side, then he has to be out seeing a patient, otherwise look out—trouble brewing."

"Your looks, Sister dear? Then I swear, he must be cross-eyed. What do you expect from those hicks anyway. Darn, I forgot his name, it's so long since I read it—Shwarl, is that it?—you know, the one who's married to Madame Bovary?"

"Little bitch? Listen to you. I'm not a little girl anymore, hahaha."

"Yes, outwardly I'm laughing, but inside it's a different story."

"Oh yes, you said you ordered a new wardrobe—and look, it's already here. Wow, *very* nice, and it's a perfect fit."

"Darn it all. I only get to visit you once in a blue moon, and looking at you two lovebirds living it up—I'm so jealous I could die."

"What—you want to buy me one? Sister, really!

그러는 건 아무렇지도 않어요.

글쎄 다 같은 한 아버지 딸에 한 어머니 태 속에서 생겨나가지굴랑, 꼭 같이 자라구 꼭 같이 공부허구 그랬으면서두 언니는 이렇게 안존허게 아무 근심 없이 사는데, 나는 하필 그이 때문에 육장[1] 애가 밭구[2] 맘이 불안허니, 그런 고루잖을 디가 어디며, 생각하면 화가 더럭더럭 난다니깐.

구식 여자들이 걸핏하면 팔자니 사주니 하는 게 아마 그런 소린가 봐. 아닌 게 아니라 미신이라두 좋으니 오늘 같어서는 어디 무꾸리[3]라두 가서 해보구 싶습디다.

그러나마 참 사람이라두 변변치 못했을세말이지, 아 유식허것다, 기개 좋것다, 무엇 굽힐 게 있수? 부모 유산 넉넉히 못 타구난 거야 어디 그이 탓이우? 돈이야 부자질 안 할 바에 기를 쓰구 모아서는 무얼 해.

애개개!

그이는 이 집 아저씨더러 하등동물이란다우. 병자 고름 긁어서 돈이나 모을 줄 알지, 세상이 곤두서건 인간이 돼지가 되건 감각두 못 허구, 그저 맛있는 음식에 좋은 옷, 편안헌 집에서 호박 같은 마나님이나 이뻐허구, 그런 것밖에는 아무것두 모른다구, 하하하. 언니두 그

Thanks but no thanks."

"No, I'm fine with the one we have. It's old but we still get some use out of it."

"I can live with being poor, that's all right with us."

"Well, I'll tell you—here we are, you and me, born of the same father, conceived in the same womb, we grew up together, went to school together, and when I see you and your peachy life, not a single worry, I think to myself, why not me? Why do I have to suffer on *his* account? My insides are churning, it's just so unfair, it makes me mad as heck!"

"I guess that's why old wives always talk about what sign you were born under, your fate, stuff like that."

"Now that you mention it, superstition or not, I almost feel like calling in a *mudang* to do her thing."

"Well, it's not as if he's crippled or something—actually he's intelligent, he's a capable man and he knows it, he doesn't have to take a back seat to anyone. He wasn't born with much of an inheritance, but is that his fault? Anyway, we'll never be rich, no matter how we try to save."

"Are you kidding—how can you say that!"

"Can you guess what he said about *your* husband? He's a lower form of life, all he knows is squeezing

런 줄은 잘 아는구려?

참, 결혼을 하면 남편 성질을 닮는다는데, 그게 정말인가 봐? 우리가 어려서는 언니가 되려 신경질루 감정이 섬세허구 잔 결벽이 유난스럽구 했는데, 그리구 나는 털펭이[4]구. 안 그랬수? 그랬는데, 시방은 꼭 반대니. 아무튼 나두 언니처럼 의사허구 결혼이나 했더라면 시방쯤 언니 부러워 않구서 엄벙덤벙 아무 근심 없이 살아갔을 거야.

네에, 옳습니다. 이번에는 내가 언니한테 졌습니다. 가치는 어디루 갔든지 간에 당장 언니가 나보담 팔자가 좋구, 그걸 내가 한편으루 부러워하는 게 사실은 사실이니깐요.

그러나저러나 대체 어떡허면 좋수? 이 일을…….

나 혼자서 두루두루 생각다 못해 이 집 아저씨허구나 상의를 좀 해볼까 허구서 부르르 오기는 왔어두, 상의를 하자면 그새 통히[5] 토설[6]을 않던 속사정을 다 자상하게 언니한테랑 설파를 해야 허겠구, 그랬다가 그런 줄을 그이가 알든지 헐 양이면 성미에 생벼락이 내릴 테구, 멀쩡한 사람 가져다 미친놈 만들려구 헌다구. 그래서 섬뻑 엄두가 나든 않지만, 그래두 어떡허우. 증세

his patients for money just like he squeezes pus out of them. The world has turned upside down, people act like animals, but what does he care? As long as he eats well, dresses nice, and has a cute, plump wife to make things comfy for him at home, everything's ducky, right? Hahaha. Don't deny it, Sis."

"Well, like they say, when you marry you start taking after your husband, yes? When we were young, *you* were the fussbudget, you were so anal and thin-skinned, and *I* was the happy-go-lucky one. Isn't that right? And now we're the exact opposite."

"The point is, if I'd married a doctor like you, Sis, I wouldn't be envying you, gee whiz, I wouldn't worry a stitch about anything."

"Yes indeed, right you are, Sister dear, this time you have won. Not in terms of values, only that you're better off than me at this moment in time. And I'm not going to hide it—there's a part of me that envies you."

"Anyway, I don't have the foggiest notion what to do. This is something—"

"I've been thinking every which way, and decided I need some advice from Brother-in-Law, so I dropped everything and rushed over here thinking

가 좀처럼 심상치 않어 뵈구, 그러니깐 도리를 좀 차리기는 차려야지만 헐 것 같은데.

이 집 아저씨 동창이든지 친구든지 누구 신경과 전문하는 이 없나 모르겠어?

신경쇠약이냐구?

그렇지, 신경쇠약은 신경쇠약이지 뭐. 그런데 시방은, 오늘버텀은 암만해두 여니 우리가 생각하는 신경쇠약에서 한 고패7)를 넘을 기미야.

언니네는 시골서 올라온 지 얼마 안 되구, 또 내가 이것저것 털어놓구 설파를 안 했구 해서 모르기두 했겠지만, 실상 나두 그새까지는 좀 심한 신경쇠약이거니, 신경쇠약으루 저만큼 심하니깐 더 도질 리야 없구 차차 나아가겠거니, 일변 걱정은 하면서두 한편으루는 낙관을 허구 있었더라우.

아, 그랬는데 글쎄 오늘은, 아까 점심 나절이야. 사람이 사뭇 십년감수를 했구려. 시방두 가끔 이렇게 가슴이 울렁거리군 하는걸. 내 원 참, 어떻게 생각하면 어처구니가 없기두 허구.

아까 그게 그러니까 두 시가 조꼼 못 돼서야. 부엌에서 무얼 좀 허구 있는 참인데 뚜벅뚜벅 구두 소리가 나요.

I'll spill it all out, all of what's happening between the two of us. I've been keeping it to myself, because if he knows, he'll start thundering at me, and I know what he's like, he'll say I'm making a sane man out as a lunatic."

"I *do* want to roll up my sleeves and get to work on him—but how? He's acting so scary I have to do *something*."

"Well, doesn't Brother-in-Law have a classmate or a friend who's a psychiatrist?"

"You think it's a neurosis?"

"Well, yes, a neurosis, kind of. But today I think he went a step beyond that."

"Sis, you're probably not aware of this, since you only moved up here a little while ago, and I haven't had a chance to lay out the whole story. I thought he'd gone downhill as far as he was going to go, he couldn't get any worse, maybe he'd even get better. So, I've been half worrying and half optimistic."

"All right, I'll tell you. This afternoon took ten years off my life, I swear. My heart's been galloping ever since. For heaven's sake, it just doesn't add up."

"It wasn't quite two o'clock. I was busy in the kitchen, and I heard him behind me."

무심결에 돌려다 봤지. 봤더니, 웬 시꺼먼 양복쟁이 야, 첨에는 몰라봤어. 그래 웬 사람인가 허구 자세 보니 깐, 그이겠지! 그이가 쇠통[8] 글쎄 겨울 양복을 꺼내 입 었어요. 이 삼복중에 겨울 양복을.

저를 어쩌니, 가 아니라 뭐 정신이 아찔하더라니깐.

그게 제정신 지닌 사람이 할 짓이우? 하얀 아사[9] 양 복을 싹 빨아 대려서 양복장에다가 걸어준 걸 두어두구 는, 이 삼복 염천에 생판 겨울 양복허구두 그나마 뭐 홈 스팡이라든지, 그 손꾸락 같이 올 굵구 시끄무레한 거, 게다가 맥고모자[10]며 흰 구두까지 멀쩡할 걸 놓아두구 서 겨울 모자에 검정 구두에 넥타이 와이셔츠꺼정 언뜻 봐두 죄다 겨울 거구려.

그러니, 그렇잖어두 늘 맘이 조마조마하던 참인데, 문 득 그 광경을 당허니 얼마나 놀랐겠수? 내가 말이야. 그 냥 가슴이 더럭 내려앉구, 어쩔 줄을 모르겠어. 팔다리 허며 입술이 사시나무 떨리듯 떨리구.

아이머니, 저이가아! 이 소리 한마디를 죽어가는 소리 루 겨우 입술만 달싹거리구는 넋이 나간 년매니루 멍하 니 섰느라니깐, 그이 좀 보구려! 마당에 우뚝 선 채 나를 마주 뻐언히 바라보더니, 아 혼자서 벌씸허구 웃겠지!

"Well, I wasn't really thinking about it, but when I wheeled around, here's this guy all dressed in black, I didn't even recognize him. Who the hell is *this*, I thought. And then I realized it was him. And he had his *winter* suit on—can you believe it? It's the dog days, for crying out loud."

"'Oh my lord'? No, Sis, it was worse than that, I practically fainted."

"Well, it's obvious, isn't it? No one in his right mind would do *that*. I'd washed and ironed his white summer suit and hung it in the wardrobe— didn't he see it? It's so steaming hot out, what's he thinking? And it wasn't his homespun, but that *black* one, the wool threads are as thick as your fingers, plus, he must have walked right past his panama hat and his white leather shoes, because instead he's wearing his fedora and his dark shoes. Add the dress shirt and the necktie, and there he was, dressed to the hilt for winter."

"Which is the last thing I need, considering my heart's always going pitty-pat these days. I mean, imagine a person like me witnessing a scene like that, what a shock it was."

"Well, my heart dropped—I mean, what was I supposed to do? I felt like a quaking aspen, I was

웃어요, 글쎄.

작년 가을 이짝 도무지 웃는 일이라구는 없던 사람이, 근 일 년 만에 웃는구료. 전에 혹시 무슨 유쾌한 일이 있든지 허면, 벌씸허구 웃던, 꼭 그런 웃음째야. 일변 반갑기두 허구, 그러면서구 가슴이 더 두군거려쌓는군. 그럴 게 아니우? 일 년짝이나 웃질 않던 사람이 갑자기 웃으니, 여편네 된 맘에 웃는 그것만은 반가워두 저이가 영영 상성[11]이 된 게 아닌가 해서 말이야.

어떻다구 맘을 진정헐 수가 없구, 눈물이 좌르르 쏟아지는 것을, 그제야 횡허케 마당으로 쫓아나가서 두 팔을 덥썩 잡았대지만, 목이 미어 말이 나오우? 그이는 내가 사색이 질려가지구는—내 얼굴이 다 죽었을 게 아니겠수? 그래가지구는 당황해허다가 끝내 울구 달려나오니깐, 첨에는 성가신 듯이 이맛살을 찌푸리더니, 용히 재갸[12] 차림새가 생각이 나던가 봐. 힐끔 아랫도리를 한번 내려다보더니 좀 점직하다는[13] 속인지, 피쓱 웃어요. 그 웃는 데 사람이 애가 더 밭더라니깐.

"왜 그래? 여름에 동복을 좀 입었기루서니, 왜 죽는 시늉이야?"

혀를 끌끌 차면서 얼굴 기색허며 말소리허며 아주 천

shivering from my lips to my toes."

"'Oh my god,' I said to myself. 'Look at him.' My voice sounded like a death rattle. I was just standing there like I'd lost my mind. And the next moment he's out in the yard, standing like a statue, eyes on me, and guess what—he flashes a grin. A grin, for god's sake!"

"No, not since last fall, not one smile in almost a year. Before that, if something pleasant happened, something that cheered him up, sure he'd grin. Just like he did in the yard."

"Of course I was glad. On the other hand, my heart was pounding like crazy. Can't you see—here's someone who hasn't cracked a smile in a year, and suddenly the smile is back. Us little women just love our smiling husband, but what if he's gone off his rocker, you know?"

"How could I calm myself down? I was crying like a river, and the next thing I knew I'd jumped down to the yard and grabbed his arms, I was so choked up. I'm sure I turned white in the face, I must have looked like death warmed over. He didn't know what to make of it, me jumping down to the yard, crying, and he made a face. Thank god he must have realized what a sight he was. He glanced

연덕스럽구 전대루지, 죄끔두 공허헌 데가 없어요. 사람이 실성을 하면 어덴지 말하는 음성이며 태도허며 건승이구 공허해 보이잖우?

"천민! 속물! 세상이 곤두서는 데는 태평이면서, 옷 좀 거꾸루 입은 건 저대지 야단이야."

속물이란 소리는 노상 듣는 독설이구, 나는 그이 눈을 주의해 보느라구 경황 중에두 정신이 없지. 저 뭣이냐, 사람이 영 미치구 나면 눈자가 틀린다구 않수?

그런데 암만 찬찬히 파구 보아야 전대루 정기가 들구 맑지, 뭐 아무렇지두 않어. 그래두 그걸루 어디 안심이 되우?

그래 팔을 잡아 흔들면서 '아이, 여보오' 부르니까,

"왜 그래 글쎄!"

하면서 보풀스럽게[14] 톡 쏘아붙이는 것까지두 여전해요.

"대체, 이 모양을 허시구 어디를 나갔다가 오시우?"

분명 어디를 나갔다가 오는 참이야. 얼굴이 버얼겋게 익구, 땀을 흠벅 흘리는 게. 탈은 거기가 붙었어, 탈은.

아아니, 그이가 글쎄 갑작스레 의관을—동복은 동복이라두—단정허게 차리구서는 출입을 허다께. 그게 사

22

down at his outfit, and it must have embarrassed him, because out came a smirk. And *that* got me burning up again."

"'What's wrong with you?' he says. 'Are you going to croak just because I'm dressed for winter in the summer?' The way he clucks—you know, *tsk-tsk*—the look on his face, his tone of voice, they're just like before, he's nonchalant as ever. Apart from the clothing and the smile, nothing's different, no holes in the armor. When someone gets deranged, there are signs, right? The way they sound, the attitude, you can see the person coming apart at the seams."

"'You're low-class!' he says to me. 'Don't be such a snob! The world's turned upside down and for you it's peace under heaven, so why the fuss if I want to dress out of season?'"

"Low-class—that's what he always says, it's like he's laying a curse on me, but I tried to forget all that while I'm giving him the hawk-eye—don't they say if someone's getting loopy, his eyes give it away?"

"No, the more I search those eyes, the more bright and shiny they look, just like before, the same spirit and energy—nothing's changed."

"A load off my mind? I *wish*."

람이 기색을 헐 노릇이 아니우? 이건 천지가 개벽을 했다면 모르지만.

그이가 작년 초가을에 신문사를 그만두던 그날버텀서 인해 일 년 짝을 굴속 같은 그 건넌방에만 처박혀 누워서는, 통히 출입이라구 하는 법이 없구, 산보가 다 뭐야, 기껏해야 화동 사는 서씨라는 친구나 닷새에 한 번큼, 열흘에 한 번큼 찾아가는 게 고작이더라우.

그러구는 허는 일이라는 게 책 들이파기, 신문 잡지 뒤지기, 그렇잖으면 끄윽 드러누워서 웃지두 않구, 이야기두 않구, 입 따악 봉허구서는 맘 내켜야 겨우 마지못해 묻는 말대답이나 허구, 그러다가는 더럭 짜증이 나가지굴랑 날 몰아세기나 허구, 그럴 때만은 여전히 웅변이지. 그러니 나만 죽어날밖에.

아, 아무 데두 맨 데가 없는 몸이것다, 좀 좋수? 집 뒤 바루 중앙학교 후원으로 해서 조금만 가면 삼청동이요, 풀이 있것다, 마침 태호 녀석이 유치원두 쉬는 때라, 동무가 없어서 어린것이 심심해 못 견디기두 허구 허니 기직[15]이나 한 닢 들구 그 애 손목이나 잡구, 매일 거기라두 가서 물에두 들어가 놀구, 물에 지치거든 그늘 좋은 솔밭으루 나와 누워서 독서두 허구, 그러노라면 몸

"Well, I grab his arms and shake him and say '*Yŏboooo!*' and he barks at me, 'What the hell!' just like he always does. And I say, 'Oh my god, where have you been, rigged out like that?'"

"*Obviously* he'd been somewhere, I mean he's red as an apple and dripping with sweat. There's something definitely wrong with him, I'm sure of it."

"Don't you see? Out of the blue, he puts on his winter suit, the whole nine yards, nice and neat and proper, and off he goes. Just looking at him scared the devil out of me. How in creation...?"

"If you ask me, it all goes back to early last fall when he quit his job at the newspaper. He's been holed up in his cave ever since, flat on his back. Go out for a walk? Heck no, he doesn't go out period! With one exception—every five or ten days he heads over to Hwa-dong to see his friend Sŏ, or so he says. And that's about it."

"Not much. Unless he's got his nose in a book or he's flipping through his newspapers and magazines, he's laid out on the floor. Regardless, there's no smiles, no talk, his mouth is clamped shut, it's all he can do to give a yes or a no, and that's only if he's in the mood, and once in a while he really gets irritated and takes it out on me, and that's the only

에두 좋구 더위두 잊구 또 아는 사람두 만나구 새루 사귀는 사람두 생기구 해서, 어우렁더우렁 만사 다 잊구 지낼 게 아니겠수? 그런 걸 글쎄, 내가 혀가 닳두룩 말을 해두 안 들어요. 냅다 날더러 신경이 둔한 속물이 돼서 자꾸만 보기 싫은 인간들허구 섭슬려[16] 돼지처럼 엄벙덤벙 지내란다구 독설이나 뱉구.

그뿐인가 뭐. 언니두 알 테지만, 집에서 어머니가 지난 첫여름버틈 벌써 네 번째나 편지를 하셨다우. 아이 아범이 올해는 아무 데두 맨 데가 없다면서 예가 바루 해변이것다, 넉넉진 못하지만 느이들이 서울서 지내느니보담야 다만 성한 생선 한 토막을 먹어두 나을 테니, 집일라컨 예서 서울 속내 잘 알구 착실한 여인네 하나가 마침 있으닌깐 올려보내서, 한여름 동안 집을 봐주게 하께시니, 부디 어린놈 데리구 세 식구 다 내려와서 이 여름 더웁잖게 지나라구, 제일에 내가 어린놈이 보구 싶어 못 살겠다구, 그리구 요전번 네 번째 하신 편지에는 혹시 여비라두 없어서 못 내려가는 줄 아시구서 내려오겠다면, 집 보아줄 사람 올려보내는 편에 돈을 얼마간 보낼 테니 곧 기별허라구까지 허셨구려.

사우[17] 이뻐할사 장모라구, 그게 다 딸이나 외손주놈

time Mr. Eloquent from the old days comes out. So here I am, the lamb before the slaughter."

"Get over what! I mean, there's nothing tying him down—he ought to feel thankful. Chungang School's right behind us, he could cut through their back garden and in no time he's at Samch'ŏng-dong and the swimming hole, and with little T'ae-ho off from kindergarten and bored out of his mind because there's no one to pal around with, he could roll up the straw mat, take the kid in hand, and off they go—just think, it's the one thing he could do any day he wanted, they can play in the water, and when they get tired, find a shady little spot beneath the pines to stretch out and he could read to the boy. It's good exercise, you can beat the heat, and besides he could see people he knows, make a new friend or two, and forget about everything under the sun—what more could you want? I've worn my tongue out trying to get him to budge, but do you think he listens! Instead he snaps at me, 'You're so obtuse, you're such a snob!' says I'm wrapped up with a bunch of jerks. He curses me saying I want him to live like a pig."

"Well, there's more to it than that. As you know, Sis, Mother's been writing us since early last sum-

보담두 실상 알구 보면 그 알뜰한 사우 양반 생각허시구, 그러시는 거 아니우? 그러니 말이우. 그렇게 살뜰스럽게 오래지 않는다구 하더래두, 딴 비발[18] 써가면서 남들은 위정 피서두 갈라더냐. 거봐요! 언니네는 갈 맘이 꿀안 같애두 못 가잖수. 그러니 글쎄 선뜻 내려갔으면 오죽 좋수?

그러나마 처가래야 처남인들 하나나 있으니, 어려운 생각이며 편안찮은 맘이 나겠수? 장인 장모 단 두 분이것다. 참말이지 재갸 본가집보담두 더 임의롭구[19] 호강 받이루 지낼 건데.

내가 얼마를 졸랐다구. 그래두 영 도래질[20]이야. 그러구는 헌댓 소리가 '나를 목을 베어봐라, 단 한 발이라두 서울서 물러서나', 이러는구려!

대체 무엇이 그다지 서울이 탐탁해서 죽어두 안 떠날 테냐구 캘라치면 '네까짓 것 하등동물이, 동아줄 신경이, 설명을 해준다구 알아들으면 제법이게? 설명해서 알 테면 설명해주기 전에 알아챌 일이지', 이러면서 몰아세요.

그러구두 졸리다 졸리다 못하면, 임자나 태호 데리구 가겠거든 가래는 거야. 웬만하거든 아주 영영 가버리라

mer, four letters by now. In the first three she keeps saying if nothing's tying him up, why not come down, there's a beach nearby, it's better than Seoul, you can get fish right off the boat, and though we aren't that well off, there's a woman we can send up to take care of the house for the summer while you're here, she's dependable, she knows her way around Seoul, and why don't we help arrange for her. She really wants us to spend the summer near the water where it's not so hot, all three of us, especially the little one, she's dying to see him. So in the latest letter, number four, that is, it sounds like she's assuming we can't go down because we can't afford it, but if we *were* to go down she'd send money for that woman to look after the house, and we should let her know right away."

"Well, we all know the mother-in-law coddles the son-in-law, more so than her daughter or her grandson, it's her precious son-in-law who's the apple of her eye, isn't it true?"

"That's what I mean. Other people are dying to get away for the summer, they spend *money* to do it. But not us—even though Mother is practically begging. Think about it, Sis. How sweet it would be if you and your family could go somewhere, but

구. 시방, 세상에 통째루 사개²¹⁾가 벙그러지는 판인데 부부구 자식이구 가정이구 그런 건 다 가버리라구. 고 담 같대나. 내 어디서 원.

왜 혼자라두 안 가느냐구 말이지? 언니두 그런 말 마 시우.

허기야 참, 몇 번 벼르기두 했더라우. 그래두 차마 훌 쩍 못 떠나가겠습디다. 그런 사람을 여기다가 떼어놔두 구서 나 혼자 가다게 될 말이우? 것도 신경이 노말한 사 람이면 몰라. 그렇지만 병인인걸, 병인을 혼자 남의 손 에 맡겨두구서야 어디.

에구 무척! 언니는 아저씨라면 들입다 깨질 똥단지 위하듯 위하면서, 하하하, 내가 그이 물이 들어서 자꾸 만 이렇게 입이 걸쭉해가나 봐.

신문사 나온 거? 뭐 누구 동료나 손윗사람허구 다투 거나 의견 충돌이 생겼던 것도 아니구, 그저 불시루 그 날 그 자리서 사직원을 써서는 편집국장 앞에다가 내놓 구 나왔다는걸. 그게 벌써 신경이 심상찮어진 표적이 아니우?

신문사서두 어디루 보구, 어떻게 생각했던지 첨에는 편지가 오구, 둘째 번은 정치부장이 오구, 셋째 번에는

you can't, right, Brother-in-Law's too busy. Wouldn't it be wonderful if we could just drop everything and go?"

"I just don't get it. There's only Mom and Dad, no brothers-in-law for him to worry about, he'd get all the pampering he needs—what's so difficult about that? To tell you the truth, he'd be a whole lot freer down there than he would with his own family."

"Oh yes, I keep after him. But he's like a little kid the way he shakes his head no. And you ought to hear him talk—'You can cut my head off but my butt's staying right here in Seoul.'"

"That's precisely what I asked him—'How come you're so in love with Seoul, that you'd rather die than leave?' Guess what? He lashes out at me: 'A lower form of life like you, a blockhead, would you understand even if I explained it to you? You're hopeless—if you can understand an explanation, then you don't need the explanation in the first place.'"

"No, when he gets sick of my pestering he tells me to get lost, says to take T'ae-ho and go down by ourselves. Or for that matter, just disappear once and for all. Now that the world's going to hell, who cares about family, marriage, children? You tell

사장의 전갈이라구 편집국장이 명함을 적어 보내구, 도루 사에 나오라는 권면이야. 그래두 번번이 몸이 건강칠 못해서 일 감당을 못 하겠다는 핑계만 대지, 종시 움쩍을 안 했더라우.

남들은 다 같이 대학을 마치구 나와서두 삼사 년씩 취직을 못 해 쩔쩔매는 세상에, 그해 동경서 나오던 멀루 신문사에 들어갔구, 인해 오 년이나 말썽 없이 있어 왔으니깐, 그만하면 신문사 인심두 얻구 또 사장두 자별하게 대접을 했답디다. 그런 것을 헌신짝 벗어 내던지듯 내던지구는 사람마저 저 지경이 됐으니…… 허기는 눈동자가 옳게 박힌 놈은 이 짓 못 해먹겠다구, 그 무렵에 바싹 더 침울해허기는 했었지만서두.

생활비?

뭐 그저, 작년 가을 겨울 두 철은 신문사서 나온 퇴직금 한 삼백 원 되는 걸루 그럭저럭 지냈구, 올봄으루 첫여름은 시댁에서 두 번인가 백 원씩 보낸 걸루 지내는 시늉은 했지만.

시댁두 별수는 없구, 막내 시아재가 작년버텀 금광을 해요. 그리 우난 건 아니지만, 동기간이 객지서 어려이 지낸다구 가끔 돈 백 원씩 그렇게 띄워 보내군 했는데,

me, Sis, have you ever heard such a thing?"

"Why not go down by myself? Sis, I wish you wouldn't talk like that."

"As a matter of fact, I've told myself that very thing, more than once."

"No—as much as I would like to, I can't simply drop everything and take off. You think I should leave him behind, the way he is? If he was a *no-mal* person—you know, *no-mal*, English *no-mal*—well, maybe. But he's a sick man, he's sick—where do I get off dumping him on someone else?"

"Sister, for god's sake! If it was *your* husband, you'd be walking on eggshells, you'd pamper him. Haha-ha, listen to me, running off at the mouth—I guess that man of mine's been rubbing off on me."

"No, it wasn't a clash with somebody or a differ-ence of opinion, he just up and quit—turned in his resignation to the editor-in-chief and left. I'd call that a distress signal, wouldn't you?"

"Well, I guess they had second thoughts. First they send him a letter, and then the political affairs editor shows up at our door, and finally the editor-in-chief mails him a business card with a message from the owner himself, and all along they're say-ing, come on back."

그 뒤에 광이 팔리기루 됐다나 봐. 팔리기만 하면은 몇만 원 생길 텐데, 매매에 걸려가지구는 두 달 장간이나 오늘내일 밀려 내려오기만 허구, 돈이 들어오덜 않는대나 봐. 그걸 바라구 있다가 우리두 고슴도치 오이 지듯 빚을 다뿍 짊어진걸.

그렇지만 괜찮아요. 영 몰리면 집은 우리 것이니깐 팔아서 빚두 가리구 한동안 먹구살 거리만 냉기구서 시외루 오막살이나 한 채 얻어 나앉지. 그런 것은 나두 뱃심 유해졌다우. 의식주 같은 건 근심하지 말구서, 돼가는 대루 살아가기루.

정말이지 그런 건 죄꼼두 걱정두 안 되구, 위협두 느끼잖아요. 그저 그이만 몸을 도루 일으켜가지구, 생화야 있든지 없든지 남처럼 활달하게 나돌아다니구 허기만 해주었으면, 뭐 내가 어디 가서 빨래품을 팔아다가 사흘에 한 끼씩 먹구 살아두 좋아요.

흰말이 아니라우. 진정이야. 그런데 글쎄, 아유 답답해! 아, 밖에 나가서 돌아다니구, 뭐 삼청동 풀에를 다니고, 피서를 떠나구, 그런 것두 외려 열두째야. 내 참!

언니두 와서 봤으니깐 알 테지만, 우리 집 건넌방이라는 게 그게 방이우? 여름 한철은 도무지 사람이 거처를

"Nope, he didn't budge, kept giving them excuses—his health isn't good, he can't handle the workload, blah blah blah."

"I mean, look at him. All these university graduates, three, four years later they still don't have a job, they're having a heck of a time, and he comes back from studying in Tokyo and the minute he arrives he lands the job with the newspaper, and in five years' time he's kept his nose clean, everybody likes him, the owner's taken him under his wing. And he throws it all away... In fact this is what he said—'Anybody with two eyes can see this is no way to make a living.' And you know, around that time he was looking absolutely miserable."

"How are we making a living? Well, we're managing. The 300 *wŏn* they sent him off with got us through last fall and winter, and this spring and then early in the summer his folks sent us 100 *wŏn*, so we put on a happy face and pretend we're scraping by."

"No—we can't depend on them. His little brother runs a gold mine, you know, but it's a small-scale enterprise. He feels sorry for his big brother, because he lives away from home too, so he sends us 100 *wŏn* from time to time. It looks now like he's

못 해요. 앞문이 정서향으루 나놔서 오정만 지나면 그 더운 볕이 쨍쨍 들이쬐지요. 게다가 처마 끝 함석 채양에서는 후끈후끈 더운 기운이 숨이 막히게 우리지요. 북창 하나 없구 겨우 마루루 샛문이 한쪽 났다는 게 바람 한 점 드나들덜 않지요. 뭐 방 속이 아니라 영락없는 한증가마 속이야. 나더러는 단 십 분을 들앉어 있으래두 죽으면 죽었지 못 해. 어느 미쟁이 녀석이 고따우루 소견머리 없이두 집을 지어놨는지.

그런 걸 글쎄 그이는 꼬박 그 속에서 배겨내는군. 가을이나 겨울이나 또 봄철은 외려 괜찮아요. 아, 이건 이 삼복중에 그 뜸가마 속에서 끄윽 들박혀 있으니, 더웁긴들 오죽허며, 여느 사람두 더위에 너무 부대끼면 신경이 약해져서 못쓰는 법인데, 이건 가뜩이나 뭣한 사람이 그 지경을 허구 있다께, 멀쩡한 자살이 아니우?

제발 마루루라두 나와서 누웠으라구, 경을 읽어두 안 들어요. 마룬들 그다지 신통헐꼬만서두, 그래두 건넌방보담은 덜허구, 또 안방은 앞뒷문으루 맞바람이 쳐서 제법 시원하다우.

단 두 내외에 어린놈 하나것다, 남의 식구라구는 없으니, 아닐 말루 활씬 벗구는 여기저기 시원한 자리루 골

fixing to sell it off, and that would probably bring him tens of thousands of *wŏn*, but there's some kind of a hangup and for a couple months now the sale keeps getting pushed back to tomorrow or the next day, and in the meantime there's no money coming in. We keep waiting, and our debts keep piling up—I feel like the porcupine with everything caught in its quills."

"Don't worry, we'll survive. If we're really hard up we can sell the house, pay off the debts, and have enough left over to live on for a while—and we could always move outside of town and get ourselves a shack. Actually I'm kind of resigned to the idea. I've decided to take things as they come and not get too worked up about how we're going to get by."

"I mean it, I don't worry that much, and I'm not threatened by the prospect. If only he can get back on his feet and get out and about, job or not, if he can do that much for me, heck, I could take in laundry, and if we only eat once in three days, well, I can handle that too."

"No lie, Sister, I'm serious. It's so frustrating! Like I said, I told him to go out somewhere, the Samch'ŏng-dong swimming hole or wherever, but at this point

라 눕던 못허우?

성가시구 다 힘이나 드는 노릇이라면, 그두 몰라. 누웠던 자리에서 몸 한 번만 뒤치면 마루루 나와지구, 또 한 번만 뒤치면 안방 뒷문 치루 옮아 누워지구 하는걸, 웬 고집이며 무슨 도섭²²⁾으루다가 고걸 꼼지락거릴라구 않구서, 생판 뜸가마 속에서만 늘어붙어설랑 육성으루 그 고생이우?

가슴이 지레 터지구, 내가 얼마나 폭폭하겠수? 사뭇 살이 내려요.

허기야 사람이 전에두 고집이 세구 신경질이 돼서 편성²³⁾이구 허기는 했지만, 시방 저러는 건 고집두 편성두 아니구서, 그저 나무토막이구 돌덩어리라니깐. 그러니 병이지, 병이 아닌 담에야 어디 그럴 법이 있수.

병원? 진찰?

흥! 그런 말만 내보우. 생사람 하나 죽구 말지 안 돼요. 안 되구, 아까 이야기하다가 말았지만, 여기 아저씨가 누구 잘 아는 이루 신경과 전문의사가 있으면 미리 짜구서, 그런 눈치 저런 눈치 뵐 게 아니라 놀러온 양으루 어물쩍하구 좀 보아달래야지, 내 억측으루는 천하 없어두 병원에는 데리구 가는 장사는 없어요.

38

that's really not a priority. Darn it all anyway!"

"Sister, you've been there, you've seen it for your-self, that *room* of his—room, how can you even call it a room? In summer it's not fit to live in. It faces due west, and by afternoon it's practically burning up in the sunlight. And with those galvanized zinc eaves, the way they overhang and heat up, it's like a steam bath. A north-facing window would be nice, but there's only that tiny little door off the veranda, so it doesn't get any breeze. It's a *cauldron* for heaven's sake. Ten minutes in there would be the death of me. The idiot who built that house, did it ever enter his thick head..."

"I don't understand it either—he just figures he'll put up with it, I guess. It's all right in fall and winter, and spring too. But now it's the *dog days*, and he won't budge from that steam pot. If the heat can wear down a healthy man, imagine what it's doing to *him*, it's like he's trying to kill himself."

"'For heaven's sake, will you *please* come out on the veranda.' I can recite that to him all day long, but do you think he listens? I know, the veranda's no miracle cure, but at least it's not as hot as that room. Plus, it gets a cross breeze if we open the door to the family room. So why can't he strip

이거 봐요, 글쎄, 오늘은 이런 재주를 다 부려보잖었겠수?

오정이 조끔 못 돼서야. 태호 벙어리를 털으니깐 제법 일 원짜리루 두 장이나 나오구, 죄다 해서 한 오육백 원은 돼요. 옳다구나, 태호허구두 구누를 해가지구서는 모자가 건넌방으루—그 양반이 농성을 허구 있는 그 한중가마 속이었다—글러루 처억 쳐들어갔구려.

들어가설랑, 아 날두 이렇게 몹시 더웁구, 이 애두 벌써 며칠째 어디를 가자구 조르구 허니깐, 우리 가서 수박두 먹을 겸, 물에두 들어갈 겸, 안양이나 잠깐 갔다가 오자구. 듣자니 사람두 그리 많지두 않구, 조용한 자리두 얼마든지 있다더라구. 뭐 있는 소리 없는 소리 주워보태가면서 은근히 추스르지를 안 했다구요. 태호는 태호대루 내가 외워준 말을 강한다는[24] 게 '안양' 먹으러 '수박' 가자구 조르구 앉었구.

첨에는 대답두 안 해요. 그래두 자꾸만 앉어서 조르니깐, 겨우 헌닷 소리가 '태호 데리구 갔다오구려', 이러는 군!

그러면서 슬며시 돌아눕는데, 글쎄 잠뱅이만 입구 알몸으루 누웠던 등허리가 땀이 어떻게두 지독으루 났든

down and make himself comfortable and find a nice cool place to lay himself—there's nobody to gawk at him except the two of us."

"Well, I could understand if it was a huge annoyance. But all he's got to do is roll over once, and he's out of his room and onto the veranda; flip over again and he's practically at the back door of the family room. But he won't move a muscle. Instead he sticks to his cauldron, it's like he wants to make things worse for himself. Either he's awfully bull-headed or he's scheming something"

"Well, my heart's about to burn a hole in my chest —I'm worrying myself silly."

"Oh yes indeed, he's always had a stubborn streak, he's not very flexible, and he's a bit eccentric, I'll grant you that, but the way he's behaving now, no way is it stubbornness or eccentricity, he's showing about as much sense as a rock or a log. Meaning he's sick—how could he not be sick and act the way he does?"

"A clinic? A checkup?"

"Hmph! I let out one little peep about getting help for him and he'll kill me, your innocent little sister. No way. Let me get back to what I was saying before—if your good husband happens to know a

지 방바닥이 홍건해요. 오죽해서 내가 걸레를 집어다가 닦었으니, 천주학이라구는!

일 그른 줄 알면서두, 그러지 말구 같이 갑시다. 당신 두 같이 가서 소풍두 허구 그래야 좋지, 우리 둘이만 무슨 재미루다가 가겠수. 자, 어서 일어나서 우선 냉수루 저 땀두 좀 씻구 그라라구 비선허듯 애기 달래듯 허니깐,

"재미?"

암말두 않구 한참 있다가 따잡듯 시비조야.

"재미라……? 게 임자네 재미 보자구 나는 고통을 받아야 하나?"

"그런 억지소릴라컨 내지두 마시우!"

나두 그제서는 속에서 부애[25]가 치밀다 못해 대구 쏠밖에.

"원, 놀러가는 게 어쩌니 고통이며, 당신 말대루 설령 고통이 된다구 합시다. 당신 좀 고통받구서, 뭐 나는 둘째야, 저 어린것 하루 실컷 즐겁게 해주면, 그게 못할 일이우?"

"그것두 천하사를 도모하는 노릇이라면……"

"에구! 그저……."

neurologist, maybe they could put their heads to-gether and cook up something, and then they drop by and see him, but not make it too obvious, in-stead they act it out, you know, 'Hey, how are you?' Because, tough as I am, under no circumstances could I wrestle him to a clinic—I'm no superwom-an, you know."

"Sister, I *have* tried. I even pulled a little trick of my own today."

"It was just before noontime, and I empty T'ae-ho's piggy bank, and what do you know, out come a couple of one-*wŏn* notes and maybe three or four *wŏn* in change. 'A jackpot!' I say to the boy and we talk hush-hush, and then over we go, mother and child, to our fine gentleman in his steam pot—he's all in a dither about something or other, but we march right in."

"Well, I say to him, 'Wow, isn't it hot, dear? You know, our boy's been pestering me for days to go somewhere—so why don't we go down to Anyang and have ourselves a watermelon and take a dip in a swimming hole? From what I hear it's not so crowded and you can find a nice quiet place just about anywhere.' I kind of pumped everything up, setting him up for T'ae-ho, but when it's time for

"……."

"글세, 여보!"

"……."

"당신 이러다가 아닐 말루 죽기나 하면 어떡허자구 그러시우?"

"헐 수 없겠지. 인간 목숨이 소중하다는 것두 요새는 전설 같아서 까마득허이!"

"드끄러워요! 내가 어디 가서 기두 맥두 없이 죽어버려야 당신이 정신을 좀 차릴려나 보우."

"얄망거리지[26] 않는 여편네는 넉넉 만큼 값이 있어. 아닌 게 아니라 아씨의 그 다변은 좀 성가셔!"

"그렇다면 아무래도 나는 죽어야 하겠구려? 당신 성가시지 않게, 또 정신을 버쩍 좀 차리게. 소원이라면 죽어드리리다."

"나를 위해서……죽는다……?"

"빈말이 아니라, 두구 봐요."

"남을 위해서 내가 죽는 것두 개죽음일 경우가 많아! 제1차 세계대전 후에 아메리카 녀석들이 무얼루 오늘날 번영을 횡재했게! 귀곡성[27]이 이천만이 합창을 하잖나! 억울하다구. 생뗴 같던 장정 이천만 명!"

the kid to say his lines, guess what the little scamp comes out with—'Let's have some *Anyang*, let's go to *watermelon*'"!

"No, it didn't get a rise out of him at all. In fact he didn't say anything at first. So I sat myself down and kept after him and finally he says, 'Go ahead, *you* take him.' Can you believe it?"

"No, he just turned over. And what a godawful sight—all he's wearing is his summer pajama bottoms and he's sweating like a hog, the sweat is dripping off his back and puddling on the floor. I had to fetch a rag and mop it up. Heaven help us!"

"I knew it wouldn't work, but I said it anyway, 'Why don't we *all* go? Some fresh air would do wonders for you. And without you it's no fun. Come on, will you *please* get up, let's get some cold water and wipe you down.' I was practically rubbing my hands together, begging that big baby."

"No, he didn't say a word, not at first. But then he says, 'Fun?' and I say to myself, Here we go, he wants to pick a fight. And he follows up with, 'Fun, huh? Fun for you two and suffering for me?'"

"Well, I'd had it by then and I couldn't help saying, 'What a mean thing to say—I wish you wouldn't force the issue. My god, since when did a family

"아이구 답답이야! 이 답답. 제에발 덕분 하느라구 저기 마루나 안방으루라두 좀 나가서 누워요. 제에발."

"그만 입 다물지 못해! 이 하등동물 같으니라고."

소리를 버럭 지르면서 되사리구 일어나 앉아요, 화가 나설랑.

"이 동물아! 내가 이렇게 꼼짝 않구서 처박혀만 있으니깐, 아무 내력 없이 그러는 줄 알아? 나는 이게 싸움이라구, 이래 봬두. 더위가 나를 볶으니까, 누가 못 견디나 보자구 맞겨누는 싸움이야, 싸움!"

내 원, 어처구니가 없어서.

더 옥신각신해야 되려 그이 신경에만 해롭겠어서 벌써 일어나 나와버렸지. 속두 상허구, 허는 깐으루는 재갸 말대루 태호나 데리구 안양이라두 곧 가겠어. 그렇지만 어디 그럴 수가 있어야지. 내가 애를 폭신 삭히구 말았지.

그러자 마침 생각하니깐 오늘이 말복이야. 그래, 온 여름 내내 그 생지옥에 처박혀 있으면서 연계[28] 한 마리두 못 얻어먹구 꼬치꼬치 야윈 게 애처롭기두 허구, 또 태호두 며칠 설사 끝에 눈이 빠꼼하구, 에라 남대문장에나 가서 연계를 두어 마리 사다가 삶어주리라구,

outing turn into suffering? Let's suppose you suffer a bit, as you say, and let's forget about me for the moment—if we give the boy a day to run free, is that too much to ask?'"

"And he says, 'A play day for the boy is supposed to make the world a better place?'"

"And I say, 'You're helpless!' He doesn't say a word. 'Come on, *yŏbo*.' Silence. And finally I say, 'Keep this up and you're going to drop dead. What then?'"

"And he says, 'When my time comes, it comes. And the notion that human life is precious is beginning to sound like a myth to me.'"

"And I say, 'Would you *please* shut up. What if *I* went *poof* somewhere! Is that what it's going to take for you to come to your senses?'"

"And he says, 'You might actually be good for something if you'd stop yapping. Frankly, my dear, chattering like you do is really aggravating.'"

"And I say, 'Well, there's the proof, I really do need to drop dead—so my dear husband won't be aggravated, and so he comes to his senses. Just say the word and I shall die for you.'"

"And he says, 'For my sake? You'd die for me?'"

"And I say, 'Try me if you think I'm joking.'"

"And he says, 'Look at all the people who died in

태호를 앞세우구 나섰지.

그이더러는 장에 가서 닭 사가지구 오마구, 좋은 말루 말을 허구 나가려니깐 되부르더니, 내려가는 길에 싸전 가게 주인더러 재갸가 엊그제 시골서 올라오기는 했는데, 일이 여의치가 못했다구, 미안헌 대루 이달 8월 그 믐꺼정만 더 참어달라구 이르라는군. 그런 걸 봐두 정신 말짱허잖수?

대놓구 먹던 아래거리 싸전에 묵은 외상값이 한 이십 원 돼요. 그걸 지난봄부터 몇 번 밀어오다가 6월 그믐껜 가는 재갸가 돈을 마련허러 시골을 내려가니, 수히 올라와서 셈을 막어주마구 그랬다는군. 그래놓구는 7월 그믐을 문두룸히[29] 넹겼는데, 글쎄 그이 허는 짓을 좀 봐요. 시골 내려갈 줄루 거짓말을 허구서는, 그담버텀은 그 앞으루 지내다니기가 안됐으니까 화동 서씨네 집을 갈 때면 곧장 내려와서 가회동으루 넘어가덜 못하구서는 위정 중앙학교 뒤루 길을 피해 비잉빙 돌아다니는 구려! 애초에 시골이니 뭣이니 할 게 아니라, 그대루 이 럭저럭 한동안 밀어가다가 생기는 날 갚어줄 것이지, 또 그래놓구서, 그 앞을 얼찐 못할 건 무엇이며, 사람이 고렇게 소심허다구는! 그런 걸 보면 천하 졸장부야.

vain for someone else. Do you have any idea why the Yankees are living high on the hog ever since World War One? Listen to the chorus of twenty million dead souls! What are they singing? "Wasted lives," that's what. Think about it—twenty million able-bodied men in the prime of life.'"

"And I tell him, 'Aigu, you're so dense, how can I get through to you! Will you *please* move yourself to the veranda, or the family room? Please.'"

"And then he barks at me, 'Can't you shut your mouth—you're such a grub.' And lo and behold, it's like he rises from the dead—he actually sits up, he's so angry. 'You imbecile! You think I *like* shutting myself up in here? Did it ever occur to you there might be a reason? You probably don't see it, but I'm involved in a *war*. It's me against the heat, and we'll see who's left standing. I'm fighting, damn it!'"

"Now can you see what I'm up against? God almighty, it's ridiculous."

"Well, all that bickering just worked him up, it was making his nerves worse, so I cleared out. My insides were churning, and the way he was behaving I thought to myself, Why not fetch up T'ae-ho and take him to Anyang, like he said. But the way he is, I couldn't leave him alone. It's such a mess, I get

그래 아무려나 시키는 대루 싸전엘 들러서 말을 그대
루 이르구는 전차를 타고 남대문장까지 가서 연계 세
마리를 털 뜯구 속 낸 걸루 사가지구 그리구 돌아오니
깐 한 시가 조꼼 못 됐더군. 아마 한 시간 남짓 했나 봐.
그런데 집에를 당도하니깐, 그이가 어디루 가구 없어
요. 집은 텅 비워놓구 대문만 지쳐두구서.

그저 짐작에 화동 서씨네 집에나 갔나보다구 심상하
게 여기구서 별 치의[30]두 안 했지. 늘 동저구리 바람으
루 시간 대중없이 주르르 가군 하니깐. 그랬지, 누가 글
쎄 동복을 지성으루 꺼내 입구, 그 야단을 떨었을 줄이
야 꿈엔들 생각했수?

그랬는데, 그래 시방 부랴부랴 닭을 삶는다, 또 그이
가 칼국수를 좋아허길래 밀가루를 반죽해 가지구 늘여
서, 썰어서, 삶어 건져놓는다, 양념을 장만한다, 거진거
진 다 돼가는 판에, 마침 들어오기는 때맞추어 잘 들어
왔다는 게 쇠통 그 모양을 해가지구 처억 들어서지를
않는다구요!

하마 조꼼 뭣했으면 내가 미칠 뻔했다우. 허겁이 아니
라 시댁두 시댁이지만 집에서 만약 어머니가 아시면 기
절을 하셨지. 그래 겨우 정신을 차려가지구, 그 얼뚱아

tired thinking about it."

"Well, it dawned on me that today's the last of the dog days. The whole summer he's been stuck in that furnace of a room, I haven't even been able to feed him a chicken to help him handle the heat, he's nothing but skin and bones, and these last few days T'ae-ho's come down with diarrhea, you ought to see his sunken eyes. For heaven's sake, I think to myself, why not go to Namdaemun Market and buy a couple of chickens—so out I go with the boy."

"Yes, I told him that, told him I was going out to buy some chickens, told him nicely, and as I was going out he calls to me. And guess what he says— I'm to tell the grain shop owner that he came back from the countryside a couple of days ago, but he's sorry, things didn't work out, and could he be patient till the end of the month? Well, that's not something a crazy man would say, is it?"

"It's down the street from us and we owe about twenty *wŏn*. We've been putting off payment since spring, and late this past June he tells the owner he's going down to the country to get some money together and he'll come right back and square things with him. But the end of July comes around and he still hasn't left, and guess what—it was all a bunch

기를 데려다가 마룻전에 걸터앉히구서 모자를 벗기구, 저구리를 벗기구, 조끼를 벗기구, 부채질을 해주구 하면서 대체 어디를 갔다가 오느냐구 재쳐 물으니깐, 종로! 종로를 갔다 온대요. 자그마치 종로를.

나는 기가 막혀서 울다가 웃었구려.

젊은이 망령은 참나무 몽둥이루 고친다는데, 이건 몽둥이질을 하잔 말두 안 나구. 아닌 게 아니라 국수를 늘이느라구 거기 마루에 놓아둔 방망이가 돌려다 보입디다!

"아아니 여보, 말쑥한 여름 양복은 두어두구서 무슨 내력으루 이걸 꺼내 입구, 종로는 또 무엇하러 가신단 말이오?"

"속 모르는 소리 말아. 이걸 떠억 입구 이걸 푸욱 눌러 쓰구, 저 이글이글한 불볕에, 어때? 온갖 인간들이 더위에 항복하는 백기 대신 최저한도루다가 엷구 시원한 옷을 입구서 그러구서 허덕허덕 쩔쩔매구 다니는 종로 한복판에 가 당당하게 겨울옷을 입구서 처억 버티구 섰는 맛이라니! 그게 어떻게 통쾌했는데!"

연설조루 팔을 내저으면서 마구 기염을 토하겠지.

"남들이 보구 웃잖습니까?"

of malarkey, and now he feels so guilty that when-
ever he visits his pal Sŏ, instead of going past the
store and straight over Kahoe-dong, he goes way
out of his way, behind Chungang School. He should
have found a better way to stall the guy. Then he
wouldn't have to feel leery about showing his tail in
front of the grain store. What do you make of a
man that timid? What it tells *me* is, he's the biggest
coward under the sun."

"Who cares, I just went to the grain store and said
what he told me to say, then I took the streetcar to
Namdaemun and bought three chickens, nice young
ones, plucked and cleaned out, and by the time I
was done it wasn't quite one o'clock—I probably
spent less than an hour there. But when I got back
home the gate was shut and the place was empty—
he was gone."

"I figured he took off to see Sŏ—nothing suspi-
cious about that. When he does go out, it's always
spur of the moment, he grabs his jacket and scur-
ries off, any hour of the day."

"So I thought, Sis. Who would have dreamed he'd
deck himself out in his winter duds, from hat to
shoes?"

"There I was running around in the kitchen, boil-

"그까짓 속충들이 뭘 알아서? 어허허, 그 친구 토옹쾌허다! 이 소리 한번 치는 놈 없구, 모두 피쓱피쓱 웃기 아니면 넋나간 놈처럼 멍허니 입을 벌리구는 쳐다보구 섰지."

보니간 그 두꺼운 양복 밖으루 땅이 뱄겠지. 얼마나 더웠어!

"그리구 참, 내 올라오면서 싸전가게 앞으루 지내와 봤는데……."

"무어랍디까?"

"그저, 안녕히 다녀오셨느냐구. 그런데 말이야, 그 앞을 지내오면서 가만히 생각하니까 썩 유쾌하겠지."

"진작 그러실 거지."

"웅, 길을 피해서 돌지두 말구, 맘을 터억 놓구서 고개를 들구서 팔을 커다랗게 치면서 그 앞을 여엿하게 지내왔단 말이야. 아주 당당히. 그래! 그게 해방이란 거야, 해방! 해방은 유쾌한 거야!"

사뭇 우줄거리는데 얼굴은 보니간, 그새처럼 침울하기는 침울해두, 말소리는 애기같이 명랑하겠지!

재갸 말대루 통쾌하구 유쾌하구 한 덕분인지 모르겠어두, 닭국에다가 국수를 말어주니간 큰 바리루 하나를

ing the chickens, kneading dough for *kalguksu*, slicing and boiling the noodles and putting them in the strainer. I put together the seasoning, and everything was pretty much ready, the only thing missing was him, and speak of the goblin, that's when he made his appearance—suddenly there he was, and you should have seen him!"

"I was at the end of my rope, any more of a shock and I would have gone over the side—and you know, Sister, I'm no shrinking violet. Sure I'm concerned for his family, but if *Mother* knew, she'd faint."

"Well, I managed to snap out of it long enough to sit that big baby down on the edge of the veranda, and I took off his hat, his jacket, his vest, I tried to cool him off with the fan, and I kept asking where in god's name he'd been, and can you believe it, he was in Chongno, right in the heart of downtown."

"I didn't know *what* to do—I was laughing and crying at the same time."

"When someone gets senile before his time, you have to fix him. Like they say, whack the oak tree with a stick. But I couldn't get the words out of my mouth. So what do I do, whack him with that rolling pin for the *kalguksu* dough, it was right there on

55

다 먹구 또 주발루 반이나 먹더군.

그러니 말이우, 그게 요행 병을 돌려서 그러는 거라면 오죽 기쁠 일이우. 그렇지만 불행히 병이 도져가는 징조라면 그 일을 장차 어떡헌단 말이우?

혈통?

없어요. 시방 당대구 선대구 그런 일은 없어요. 아니야, 내가 글쎄 그이허구 결혼헌 지가 칠 년인데, 그이 학부 마칠 동안 삼 년허구 취직한 뒤에 살림 시작하기 전 이 년허구, 오 년이나 시댁에서 지냈는걸. 아무런들 그이 집안에 정신병 혈통이 있는지 없는지 몰랐겠수?

옳아, 언니 시방 하는 말이 맞었어. 나두 실상 그렇게 짐작은 했다우. 그러니 말이지, 사내대장부가 어찌 그대지 못났수? 이건 과천서 뺨 맞구, 서울 와서 눈 흘기기 아니우? 젠장맞을, 차라리 뛰쳐나서서 냅다 한바탕…… 응? 그럴 것이지, 그렇잖수?

그러구저러구 간에 시방 나루서는 병 시초나 또 뿌렁구[31]나 그게 문제가 아니야. 다못 그이가 정말루 못쓰게 신경 고장이 생겼느냐, 요행 일시적이냐, 만약에 중한 고장이라면 어떻게 해야만 그걸 나수어주겠느냐, 이것 뿐이지. 그밖에는 아무것두 내가 참견할 게 아니야. 날

the veranda where I'd put it."

"So I say to him, '*Yŏbo*, you've got a nice neat summer suit, whatever made you take out *that* one, and *what* were you doing in Chongno?'"

"And he says, 'Don't talk like an ignoramus. So what if I go out in *this* suit and *this* hat and fry in the sun? You want me to be like all those clowns who raise the white flag and surrender to the heat? You ought to see them, huffing and puffing, and they're hardly wearing *anything*. Me, I go smack dab to the center of Chongno, in my winter clothes, and stake out a place there—did *that* feel good! I was proud of myself. It was absolutely triumphant!'"

"What a blowhard, waving his arms around and putting on a show."

"So I say, 'No one laughed at you?'"

"And he says, 'What do those worms know? I was kind of hoping somebody might say, "Look at this guy, now *that's* style for you." But no, not a one of them, the sons of bitches. If they weren't smirking at me, they were looking up with their jaws hanging open wondering if I was out of my mind.'"

"And then I noticed his suit jacket was practically oozing sweat—imagine, he must have been boiling."

더러 그이를 이해를 못 한다구? 딴전을 보구 있네! 그게

어디 이해를 못 허는 거유?

　마침 맞게 아저씨가 들어오시는군.

　내친 걸음이니 아무려나 같이 앉아서 상의를 좀 해보

구…….

1) 육장. 한 번도 빼지 않고 늘.
2) 밭다. 근심, 걱정 따위로 몹시 안타깝고 조마조마해지다.
3) 무꾸리. 무당이나 판수에게 가서 길흉을 알아보거나 무당이나
　　판수가 길흉을 점침.
4) 털펭이. 덜렁이.
5) 통히. '도무지' '아무리 해도'
6) 토설. 숨겼던 사실을 비로소 밝히어 말함.
7) 고패. 일정한 두 곳 사이를 한 번 오고가는 것을 세는 단위.
8) 쇠통. '온통'의 방언(경기, 함남).
9) 아사. 삼베.
10) 맥고모자. 맥고로 만든 모자. 개화기에 젊은 남자들이 주로
　　썼다. 밀짚모자.
11) 상성. 본래의 성질을 잃어버리고 전혀 다른 사람처럼 됨.
12) 재갸. 자갸. 자기를 조금 높여 이르는 말.
13) 점직하다. 부끄럽고 미안하다.
14) 보풀스럽게. 모질고 날카롭게.
15) 기직. 왕골껍질이나 부들 잎으로 짚을 싸서 엮은 돗자리.
16) 섭슬리다. 함께 섞여 휩쓸리다.
17) 사우. 사위.
18) 비발. 비용.
19) 임의롭다. 일정한 기준이나 원칙이 없어 하고 싶은 대로 할
　　수 있다.
20) 도래질. 도리질.
21) 사개. 상자 따위의 모퉁이를 끼워 맞추기 위하여 서로 맞물리
　　는 끝을 들쭉날쭉하게 파낸 부분.
22) 도섭. 주책없이 능청맞고 수선스럽게 변덕을 부리는 짓.
23) 편성. 한쪽으로 치우친 성질.

"And then he says, "Oh, and you'll get a kick out of this—on the way home I thought I'd swagger right past the grain store.""

"And I say, "What did they say?""

"And he says, 'Nothing much, just "Hello, having a good day?" And I thought to myself, Now that's more like it.""

"And I say, 'You should have done that in the first place.""

"And he says, 'Yeah, maybe you're right. No detour this time, I just took it easy, held my head high, marched right past the place carefree as all hell, and proud as could be. You bet! What a feeling of liberation! I tell you, liberation feels *good!*""

"Oh he was full of himself all right. Still had some of that hangdog look, but overall he was cheerful as a baby."

"Maybe it was that triumphant feeling, or just that he felt *good*, but after I added the chicken broth to the *kalguksu* he ate a whole bowl full—out of my little bowl—then half a bowl more out of his big bowl."

"You know, I can't be sure. If he's turning the corner, then great! But if it's a sign of a relapse, then what?"

24) 강하다. 예전에, 서당이나 글방 같은 데서 배운 글을 선생이
    나 시관 또는 웃어른 앞에서 외다.
25) 부애. '부아(노엽거나 분한 마음)'을 나타내는 경상도 사투리.
26) 얄망거리는. 지나치게 약삭빠르고 까다로운.
27) 귀곡성. 귀신의 울음소리.
28) 연계. '영계'의 원말.
29) 문두룸히. 우두커니 하는 일 없이.
30) 치의(致疑). 의심을 둠.
31) 뿌렁구. '뿌리'의 방언(경남, 전남).

* 작가 고유의 문체나 당시 쓰이던 용어를 그대로 살려 원문에
  최대한 가깝게 표기하고자 하였다. 단, 현재 쓰이지 않는 말이
  나 띄어쓰기는 현행 맞춤법에 맞게 표기하였다.

《조광(朝光)》, 1938

"In his family? No, not in his lifetime, and not in his ancestors either. You know, it's seven years we've been married, but I lived with his family the three years he was in school and the first two years after he got a job—that makes five years—and don't you think I'd know after that if insanity runs in his family?"

"Right you are, Sister, yes. Actually I thought about that too. He's not a man's man, that's for sure—talk about getting slapped around in Kwach'ŏn and not bitching about it till you get to Seoul. Darn it all anyway. Why can't he just go out and show the world who's boss, huh? That's what he should do, right?"

"As far as I'm concerned, the issue now isn't how he got sick in the first place or what the root cause is."

"What *I* want to know is, is he beyond hope, or is it just temporary? And if he really *is* having a breakdown, then how can I make him better? Beyond that, I don't see where I can stick my nose in. And you're telling me I don't understand him? Where have you been all this time—haven't you been listening? How could I *not* understand him?"

"Well, guess who's here—and it's about time."

"As long as I've dragged my rear end all the way over here, why can't I sit myself down with him and pick his brain, then we take it from there?"

Translated by Bruce and Ju-Chan Fulton

해설

Afterword

내 소원을 들어줄 지니

브루스 풀턴

(브리티시 컬럼비아 대학교, 한국문학 및 문학번역, 민영빈 석좌교수)

「소망(少妄)」은 문예지《조광》1938년 10월호에 처음으로 발표되었다. '소망'이라는 제목은 소년(少年)이라는 말과 노망(老妄)이라는 말의 합성어로, 이 이야기에 나오는 비교적 젊은 남자가 그의 선량한 아내의 눈에 조기 노망의 증상을 보이고 있는 것으로 보인다는 점을 지적하려고 작가 채만식이 사용한 말로 보인다.

그러나 채만식이 '소망'이라는 제목을 만들면서 이 단어의 동음이의어 두 가지를 염두에 두고 있었을지도 모른다는 가능성을 간과할 수는 없다. 즉 '욕망', '소원', '희망', '기대' 등을 뜻하는 소망(所望)이 그 하나이며, 그보다 더 강렬한 의미의 동의어로 '마음속 깊이 품고 있는

Genie for My Hopes

Bruce Fulton

(Young-Bin Min Chair in Korean Literature and Literary Translation,
University of British Columbia)

"Juvesenility" (Somang, 소망 [少妄]) was first published in the October 1938 issue of *Chogwang* (Light
of Chosŏn). The title "少妄" is a portmanteau word
derived from the words *sonyŏn* (少年, boy, youth) and
nomang (老妄, senility, dotage), presumably used by
author Ch'ae Man-Sik to indicate that the husband
in the story, a relatively young man, may in the eyes
of his good wife, the narrator, be showing early
symptoms of dementia. But we must also consider
the possibility that in creating this title Ch'ae also
meant to echo two homonyms of that word, the *somang* (所望) meaning "desire, wish, hope, expecta-
tion," and its more intensive synonym, the *somang*

갈망' 혹은 '가장 소중한 꿈'을 뜻하는 소망(素望)이 그 다른 하나이다.

현재 활동 중인 케이팝 그룹 소녀시대 인기의 많은 부분이 그들의 초자연적인 노래 「소원을 말해봐」와 그 노래의 2개 국어로 된 후렴구, 즉 "소원을 말해봐, I'm Genie for you, boy; 소원을 말해봐, I'm Genie for your wish; 소원을 말해봐, I'm Genie for your dream; 내게만 말해봐, I'm Genie for your world"에 힘입은 바 크다고 본다. 여기서 소원(所願)이라는 단어는 채만식의 소설 제목과 동음이의어인 소망(素望)이라는 말과 흡사한 의미를 지닌다.

위트나 상상력이라는 면에서 채만식은 아마도 근대 한국 작가 중 이상을 제외하면 단연 으뜸일 것이고, 그런 그는 새 천년의 한 한국 팝송이 그의 소설과 의미상 상호연관성을 띠고 있을지도 모른다는 가능성에 미소 지을 것이 분명하다.

그러나 우리가 채만식의 소설 중 몇 가지, 예를 들자면 「치숙」(1938), 「맹순사」(1946), 「처자」(1948) 등에서 아내들이 그들의 남편들에 대해 큰 희망을 품고 있는 것처럼 보인다는 점을 고려해 볼 때, 그 연관성은 상당한

(素望) meaning "one's heart's desire" or "one's dream of dreams."

Much of the popularity of the contemporary K-pop group Girls Generation (소녀시대) owes to its transcendental song "Genie" (Sowŏn ŭl malhaeboa, 소원을 말해봐) and its bilingual refrain: "소원을 말해봐, I'm Genie for you, boy; 소원을 말해봐, I'm Genie for your wish; 소원을 말해봐, I'm Genie for your dream; 내게만 말해봐, I'm Genie for your world." The wish or dream in question is *sowŏn* (所願) in Korean, which is almost identical to the *somang* (素望, one's heart's desire) that is a homonym of the title of Ch'ae's story.

Ch'ae Man-Sik, perhaps second only to Yi Sang among modern Korean writers in terms of wit and imagination, would certainly smile at the possibility of a new millennium Korean pop song serving as a point of intertextual reference for his story. But the connection is instructive if we consider that in several of Ch'ae's stories, such as "My Innocent Uncle" (Ch'isuk 치숙, 1938), "Constable Maeng" (Maeng sunsa 맹순사, 1946), and "The Wife and Children" (Ch'ŏja 처자, 1948), the wife appears to hold out high hopes for her husband. And why not? The husband in both "My Innocent Uncle" (that is, the uncle of the narrator)

의미를 가진다.

사실 이야기 속의 아내들은 그렇게 기대할 만한 충분한 이유가 있다. 「치숙」에 나오는 남편(화자의 삼촌)과 「처자」에 나오는 남편은 모두 교육을 받은 지식인이고, 그 사실은 1930년대만 해도 문맹률이 약 90퍼센트에 달하던 한국사회에서는 아주 드문 일이었다. 그리고 「맹순사」에 등장하는 남편은 일제 강점기와 해방 후 남한의 미군정 기간 중 요직이었던 경찰의 일원이다.

「소망」에서 아내는, 남편이 걱정 없는 삶을 살고 싶다는 그녀의 소망을 실현시켜줄 것이라는 열렬한 희망을 품고 있다. 그녀가 그렇게 기대하고 있는 지니 같은 남편은 일본에서 받은 고등교육, 서울 모 신문사의 직장, 그들 부부와 그들의 어린 아들까지를 경제적으로 돕고 있는 부모, 금광 소유자인 형, 서울의 노른자 동네 삼청동 근처에 위치한 집 등 모든 자격 조건을 갖추고 있다.

그런데 어느 날 그는 갑자기 신문사에 사직서를 내고, 그를 다시 불러들이려는 모든 시도에 저항한다. 그 이유는 무엇일까? 그는 전쟁을 하고 있는 것이다. 여기서 전쟁을 한다는 것은 그가 그의 집의 동굴 같은 한 방에 스스로를 가두는 것을 말한다. 이 점, 고려와 조선시대

and "The Wife and Children" is an educated man and an intellectual, a rarity in a society that as recently as the 1930s had an illiteracy rate estimated at 90 percent. And the husband in "Constable Maeng" is a member of the all-important constabulary during the Japanese colonial period and the American military government that succeeded it in southern Korea after Liberation.

The ardent hope of the wife in "Juvesenility" is that her husband will fulfill her hopes of living a worry-free life. Her hoped-for genie of a husband has all the credentials—higher education in Japan, a job at a newspaper in Seoul, parents who support the couple and their young son financially, a brother who owns a gold mine, a home near the choice neighborhood of Samch'ŏng-dong in Seoul. And then one day he abruptly resigns from the newspaper, and resists all attempts to lure him back. His reason? He's involved in a "war." And waging that war means locking himself up in his "cave" of a room at home—not unlike the scholar-officials of Koryŏ and Chosŏn times who retired to the countryside rather than participate in a life in the capital that they considered corrupt.

The war our hero is fighting is ostensibly with the

에 부패한 수도에서의 삶에 참여하기보다 차라리 관직을 버리고 낙향을 감행했던 선비 관리들과 과히 다르지 않다. 외면상으로 주인공은 여름철 삼복더위와 전쟁을 치르고 있다. 이열치열이라고, 그는 두꺼운 겨울옷을 껴입고 서울 도심이라는 전선에서 전투 준비 완료 상태의 자신을 과시하고 있다. 그러나 사실상 그가 싸우고 있는 대상은 식민지 한국에서의 지식인들의 진부한 기성적 삶인 것이다. 이것은 채만식이 그의 걸작 소설인 「레디메이드 인생」(1934) 그리고 「치숙」에서 풍자한 삶과 같은 맥락이다. 여기서 기성적 삶이란, 태생이 좋은 젊은 한국 남자들은 당연히 일본에서 고등교육을 마치고 한국으로 돌아와 급속히 근대화하고 있는 식민지 사회에서 전문직 종사자로 자리를 잡도록 기대되고 있다는 의미에서의 진부한 삶을 말하고 있다. 이것은 작가 자신이 1950년 그의 생을 마감할 때까지 끈질기게 싸우게 될 바로 그 전쟁이었다. 그의 자전적 중편소설 「민족의 죄인」(1948~49)에서 주인공은 식민지 시대의 성공적인 작가로서의 자신의 정치적 자세를 재평가하려고 시도한다.

「소망」에 등장하는 남편은 처음에는 교육받은 식민지

heat of dog-day summer. Fighting heat with heat, he dons his thick winter clothing to display himself in fighting trim all alone on the front lines of downtown Seoul. But the war he is actually fighting is against the ready-made life of the intellectual in colonial Korea, a life Ch'ae Man-Sik lampooned in his classic stories "A Ready-Made Life" (Redimeidŭ insaeng 레디메이드 인생, 1934) and "My Innocent Uncle"—a life ready-made in the sense that wellborn young Korean men were expected to complete their higher education in Japan and return to Korea to take their place as professionals in a rapidly modernizing colonial society. This was a war that the author himself would continue to fight until his death in 1950: in his autobiographical novella "An Enemy of the People" (Minjok ŭi choein 민족의 죄인, 1948~49) the protagonist attempts to reevaluate his political posture as a successful writer during the colonial period.

In "Juvesenility," the husband initially buys into the ready-made life dangled before educated Korean colonial subjects. But when he opts out of that life, having realized that "the world has turned upside down," and goes to "war," 5 years into his job with the newspaper, it is his wife, the narrator of the

한국인들을 유혹하는 레디메이드 인생에 영합한다. 그러나 신문사 근무 5년 만에 "세상이 곤두서 뒤집혀버렸다"는 것을 깨닫고서 기존의 삶을 떠나 "전쟁"을 시작할 무렵, 다름 아닌 바로 이 소설의 화자인 그의 아내가 이미 그의 뒤를 이어 자신의 희망과 꿈의 초점을 레디메이드 삶에 맞추게 되어버렸다. 그것은 이미 그녀의 언니와 의사인 형부가 성취한 삶이고, 화자는 그 잉꼬부부와 그들의 장밋빛 인생을 선망한다. 그녀는 남편이 지식인이며 유능한 남자로서, 만일 그가 "정상적"이기만 하다면 그가 "태평천하"라고 빈정대는 바로 그 레디메이드 인생을 그녀에게 가져다줄 수 있는 사람이라고 생각한다(채만식의 가장 성공적인 작품이라 할 수 있는 소설의 제목도 『태평천하』(1938)이다).

그러나 화자의 숙원을 이루어줄 지니가 되는 대신에, 남편은 식민지 시대의 한국 소설에 줄지어 등장하는 몰락한 지식인들의 대열에 합류한다. 그 대열에는 이미 현진건의 「술 권하는 사회」(1921)의 술주정뱅이 남편, 이태준의 「까마귀」(1936)의 특이한 작가, 이상의 「날개」(1936)의 고지식하고 불안정한 화자, 그리고 「치숙」의 병적인 삼촌 등이 속해 있었다.

story, who has succeeded him in focusing her hopes and her dreams on that life. It is a life already achieved by her sister and brother-in-law, a doctor: she is jealous of the "two lovebirds" and their "peachy life." She considers her own husband an intelligent and capable man, who if only he were "normal" could gain for her a life he sarcastically describes as "peace under heaven" (the title of what is arguably Ch'ae's most accomplished novel, *T'aep'yŏng ch'ŏnha* 태평천하, 1938).

So instead of being a genie for the narrator's cherished hopes, the husband joins the ranks of the ruined intellectuals who parade through the fiction of colonial Korea—the alcoholic husband in Hyŏn Chingŏn's "A Society That Drives You to Drink" (Sul kwŏnhanŭn sahoe 술 권하는 사회, 1921), the idiosyncratic author in Yi T'ae-jun's "Crows" (Kkamagwi 까마귀, 1936), the naïve and unstable narrator of Yi Sang's "Wings" (Nalgae 날개, 1936), and the tubercular uncle in "My Innocent Uncle." Unwilling or unable to compromise with the prevailing political, ideological, cultural, or artistic winds, they present the look of those who are demented before their time, the genie of imperial Japan appearing tarnished in their eyes and rendering them incapable of realizing the

당시의 유력한 정치적, 이념적, 문화적, 혹은 예술적 경향과 타협을 꺼리거나 타협할 수 없었던 그들은, 조기 노망한 인물들의 모습, 즉 그들의 눈에 타락자로 비치는, 또 그들로 하여금 그들의 가족, 사회, 혹은 조국의 꿈과 희망을 실현시킬 수 없도록 만드는 제국주의 일본의 지니로서의 모습을 제시한다.

채만식에 대한 학술적 글들은 식민지 사회의 모순을 고발하는 그의 지극히 발달된 풍자 기술을 강조하는 경향이 있다. 그러나 여성이 그들의 삶에서 경제적으로, 지적으로 남성에 의존하는 경향을 낳았던 신 유교적 성차별 관념의 지속적인 영향이 그의 작품 속에 존재한다는 사실은 비교적 적은 관심을 받고 있다. 그렇다면 채만식 소설 속의 아내들이 잠재적 능력을 갖춘 남편들을, 그들이 소원해 온 물질적, 정서적 위안을 가져다줄 지니라고 생각하는 것도 별로 놀랄 일은 아니지 않을까?

hopes and dreams of their family, society, or nation.

Scholarly writing on Ch'ae Man-Sik tends to emphasize his highly developed skill in satirizing the contradictions of colonial society. Less attention is paid to the presence in his fictional works of the ongoing influence of neo-Confucian gender ideology, a result of which was that women tended to be dependent both economically and intellectually on the men in their lives. Is it any wonder that they saw in their potentially capable husbands a genie who would provide them with whatever material and emotional comfort they may have hoped for?

비평의 목소리

Critical Acclaim

(……) 채만식의 「소망」에서는 뜻있는 한 인텔리 청년의 성격파탄스런 행위를 통하여 신랄하게 일제의 식민통치에 항거하고 시대를 부정하는 우회공격의 지혜를 엿볼 수 있다. 갑자기 스스로 신문사에 사표를 낸 주인공(그이)이 굴 속 같은 건넌방에 처박힌 채 삼복더위의 뜸가마 속에서 책을 벗하면서 "나는 이게 싸움이야……싸움" 하고 말한다. 그러다가 이따금 한여름에 동복을 갖추어 입고 온갖 인간들의 더위에 항복하는 백기 대신 종로 한복판을 활보하고 와서 당당히 소리치는 것이다. 세상이 곤두서는데 태평이면서, 옷 좀 거꾸로 입는 건 아우성이냐며 천민! 속물이라 통박하는 것은 작중의 화

[...] In "Juvesenility" readers can sample the wisdom of indirect criticism through the abnormal behavior of a righteous young intellectual who bitingly protests colonial Japanese rule and opposes the trends of the times. Suddenly quitting his newspaper job, he holes up in his cavern-like room, with books as his only companion, during the steam pot of the dog days, barking at his wife, "I'm involved in a *war*. I'm fighting, damn it!" Dressing up from time to time in his winter suit and swaggering to the heart of downtown, he refuses to follow everyone else in waving the white flag of surrender to the heat, returning home instead to trumpet to his wife,

자인 아내가 걱정하듯 정신이상이 아닌, 매섭고 효과적인 항일의지의 표출이다. 이 경우 햇빛이나 무더위는 일제의 횡포한 통치를 암시한 것이며 거기에 굽히지 않고 겨울옷으로 버티고 활보하는 행위는 해학성을 지닌 풍자의 하나라 여겨진다. 어떻게 보면, 이들의 작품에는 일제에 대하는 풍자적 저항이 너무 약하게 느껴져서 (……) 시종 철저한 식민지 통치를 전횡해 온 당시의 문학외적인 상황을 고려한다면 언어와 문자를 통하여 활자화하는 과정에서 검열제도의 난관을 거쳐야 한다는 사정을 감안할 때 우리는 그들 문인의 고충을 충분히 이해해둠이 필요하다.

이명재, 『식민지시대의 한국문학』, 중앙대학교 출판부,
1991, 145~46쪽

이런 서술자의 진술은 역논리이거나 반어적인 성격이 강하여 오히려 서술자 자신이 풍자의 대상이 되기 때문에, 작가의 현실 비판의식을 간접적이면서도 효과적으로 전달하는 서술방식으로 자리 잡을 수 있었다. 채만식의 「치숙」과 「소망」에 나오는 서술자가 여기에 해당될 수 있는데, 작가는 이런 서술자의 설정으로 식

"You're low-class!... Don't be such a snob! The world's turned upside down and for you it's peace under heaven, so why the fuss if I want to dress out of season?" Though his wife considers his behavior a manifestation of mental illness, it is a virulently effective expression of anti-Japanese will. The blazing sun and the sultriness of the season are metaphors for tyrannical Japanese colonial rule, and his undefeated strut in his winter suit is satire replete with humor. No matter how we consider such works, the satirical resistance they convey against Japanese rule feels weak. [...] However, if we take into account that all Korean-language print material underwent censorship as part of Japan's steadfast and exhaustive policies governing matters extra-literary as well as literary, we necessarily understand more fully the predicament of the writers of that period.

Yi Myŏng-jae, *Korean Literature during the Colonial Period*,
Chungang University Press, 1991, pp. 145~46

Because the narrator's statements appear to be illogical or ironic and the narrator himself becomes a target of satire, the use of an effective indirect-narrative style makes possible the delivery of the writ-

민지 체제가 자리 잡혀가던 1930년대의 가치혼란 현상을 잘 드러내고 있다. (……) 「소망」 역시 세속적이고 상황적 진실에 무지한 1인칭 서술자가 남편의 기행에 담긴 참뜻을 이해하지 못하여 자신의 무지와 속물스러움을 폭로하고 있는 작품이다. (……) 남편의 비정상적인 행동은 '곤두선' 현실을 살아가기 위해서는 자기 자신도 '곤두선' 상태를 갖출 수밖에 없다는 자기 신조에서 비롯된 것이므로, 작가가 이러한 인물을 통하여 그 시대의 불건강성과 왜곡됨을 함축적으로 이야기하고 있다는 것을 알 수가 있다.

이수정, 『현대소설 시점의 시학』, 새문사, 1996, 181~82쪽

역사의 진보를 이룩해 내는 허구의 신이 사라져 버린 시대에 [작가는] 비극적 현실의 연원(역사)을 밝히거나 그 현실의 모순을 폭로하는 작업으로 모아 (……) 현실성이면서 동시에 부정성인 대상을 (……) 역설 혹은 아이러니로서의 풍자의 미학이 생성되는 지점이 바로 이 지점이다. 폭로와 동시에 부정인 미학, 그것이 곧 역설 혹은 아이러니로서의 풍자의 방법적, 미학적 요체인 셈이다. 개진과 동시에 부정이라는 점에서 그것은 역설인

er's critique of contemporary reality. The narrators of "My Innocent Uncle" and "Juvesenility" are examples of this narrative style, enabling Ch'ae Man-Sik to describe effectively the chaotic value system of the 1930s, when the colonial government was entrenched. [...] In "Juvesenility" the philistine first-person narrator reveals her snobbery and her ignorance of reality through her failure to understand her husband's eccentricity. [...] Her husband's abnormal behavior derives from his creed that to survive in an upside-down world he too must act upside-down, a statement that carries overtones of ill health and distorted reality.

Lee Su-jeong, *The Poetics of Perspective in Modern Fiction*,

Saemunsa, 1996, pp.181~82

At a time when the fictitious god of historical progress has vanished, [the author] focuses his work on revealing the tragic origins (history) of reality or exposing its contradictions. [...] Subjects that are realistic and at the same time pessimistic [...] constitute the very juncture at which an aesthetics of paradox and ironical satire is created. It would seem that an aesthetics of disclosure and at

것이며 비판과 동시에 웃음이라는 점에서 그것은 풍자인 것이다. 이 점을 집약적으로 드러내고 있는 진술이 다름 아닌 '잘난 사람들'(즉 못된 잘난 사람들)인 셈이다.

한형구, 「한국근대문학의 탐구」, 태학사, 1999, 394-95쪽

the same time pessimism is methodically the key factor in satire that is precise, paradoxical, and ironic. It is paradoxical in stating and at the same time negating, and satirical in criticizing and at the same time laughing. And it would seem that the collective statements on this point are made by none other than the [individuals Ch'ae Man-Sik referred to as] "bright bulbs" (who in actuality are dim bulbs).

Han Hyŏng-gu, *A Study on Modern Korean Literature*,

T'aehaksa, 1999, pp. 394-95

채만식

소설가이자 극작가, 수필가, 평론가를 겸했던 채만식
은 전라북도의 한 바닷가 마을인 읍내에서 1902년에 태
어났다. 그 세대의 많은 지식인들이 그랬듯이, 그도 한
동안 일본의 와세다대학교에서 수학한 후, 고국으로 돌
아와 일련의 집필과 편집 활동을 했다. 1936년부터 그
가 결핵으로 사망한 1950년까지 그는 꾸준히 본격적인
집필에 몰두했다.

채만식은 근대 한국문학의 훌륭한 인재 중의 한 사람
이었다. 그의 뛰어난 통찰력, 어휘 구사력, 너무나도 실
감나는 대화체, 그리고 예리한 재치는 채만식으로 하여
금 그만의 소설적 스타일을 만들어내게 해주었다.

그의 이야기들 중에는 화자가 독자에게 직접 이야기
를 들려주는 것 같은 즉시성을 느끼게 하는 소설들이
있는데, 그 점은 이야기 판소리의 구비 전통을 상기시
켜 주기도 한다. 채만식은 또한 그 자신의 뿌리를 반영
하는 듯 시골의 궁핍함에 대한 묘사, 또 일제 강점기에
물질적으로는 풍족하나 정신적으로는 메말라 있었던

Ch'ae Man-Sik

Ch'ae Man-Sik—fiction writer, playwright, essay-
ist, critic—was born in Ŭmnae, a coastal village in
North Jeolla Province, in 1902. Like many of the intellectuals of his generation, he studied for a time in
Japan, at Waseda University, then returned to Korea
to work at a succession of writing and editorial
jobs. He worked full time at writing from 1936 until
his death from tuberculosis in 1950.

Ch'ae is one of the great talents of modern Korean literature. His penetrating mind, command of id-
iom, utterly realistic dialogue, and keen wit pro-
duced a fictional style all his own. The immediacy
of some of his narratives, the sense of the storytell-
er speaking directly to the reader, is reminiscent of
the traditional oral narrative *p'ansori*.

Ch'ae is equally skilled at portraying the poverty
of the countryside (reflecting his own roots), the sump-
tuous lifestyle of those Koreans who flourished
materially yet withered spiritually during the Japanese occupation, and the new class of young, ur-

계층의 한국인들의 사치스러운 생활양식, 그리고 식민지시대에 출세의 길이 너무도 한정되어 있던 신세대의 젊은 도시 지식인들의 묘사에도 능숙하다.

그는 1945년 해방 이전이나 이후에도 변함없이 활동했던 비교적 소수의 20세기 한국 소설가들 중 하나이기도 하다. 그래서 우리는 그의 이력을 통해 일제의 식민통치하에서 한국인이 겪은 곤경, 그리고 해방 후 닥쳐온 식민통치의 여파를 들여다 볼 수 있는 진귀한 창을 얻게 된다.

채만식은 일반적으로 「레디메이드 인생」(1934), 「치숙」(1938), 「미스터 방」(1946) 등의 작품을 쓴 풍자가로 알려져 있다. 「치숙」은 일제하의 사회에 적응 불가능한 한 사회주의자와 그의 기회주의적 조카를 중심인물로 하는 이야기이고, 「미스터 방」은 해방 후 남한에서의 미군정 시기를 배경으로 하고 있다. 그러나 풍자가라는 협소한 관점만을 고집한다면 채만식의 폭넓은 작품 세계에 대한 공정한 평가는 될 수 없을 것이다.

1923년에 완성되었으나 1973년이 되어서야 발표된 「과도기」는 그의 알려진 작품 중에서 최초의 것으로, 20세기 초 동아시아의 도시를 휩쓸었던 근대화의 물결을

ban intellectuals whose career horizons were so limited during the colonial era. He is also one of the relatively few twentieth-century Korean fiction writers to have been active both before and after Liberation in 1945. His career thus lends us a rare perspective on the difficulties of Koreans under Japanese colonial rule and the aftereffects of that rule following Liberation.

Ch'ae is usually thought of as a satirist, on the basis of stories such as "A Ready-Made Life" (Redimeidŭ insaeng 레디메이드 인생, 1934) and "My Innocent Uncle" (Ch'isuk 치숙, 1938), the latter focusing on a socialist misfit and his opportunistic nephew during the Japanese occupation, and "Mister Pang" (Misŭt'ŏ Pang 미스 터 방, 1946), set during the American military occupation of the southern sector of post-Liberation Korea. Such a narrow characterization, though, does not do justice to the breadth of Ch'ae's writing. His earliest known work, "Age of Transition" (Kwadogi 과 도기, written in 1923 but not published until 1973), is an autobiographical novella about Korean students in Japan testing the currents of modernization that swept urban East Asia early in this century. His first published work, "In Three Directions" (Se killo 세 길 로, 1924), concerns three young intellectuals about

시험해 보고 있는 일본에 있는 한국인 유학생들을 그린 자전적 중편소설이다. 그가 최초로 발표한 소설「세 길로」(1924)는 막 출세의 가도에 오르려 하는 세 명의 젊은 지식인, 그리고 예나 지금이나 항상 한국사회에서 뚜렷이 존재하는 사회계층 간의 불화를 다룬 작품이다.

1920년대와 1930년대에 발표된 채만식의 소설들은 당시 식민지 한국의 근대화 운동에 의하여 생겨난 무직의 젊은 지식인의 곤경에 좀 더 각별한 초점을 맞추고 있다. 작가는 출판사와 전당포를 전전하며 살아가는 무일푼의 젊은 지식인들을「레디메이드 인생」에서 통렬한 정확성을 가지고 묘사하고 있다.

1930년대 말에 발표된 두 개의 소설은 그의 가장 중요한 작품에 속한다. 그중 하나가『태평천하』(1938)로 일제 강점기에 물질적으로는 풍요하나 정신적으로는 피폐한 한 인물을 통하여 한국의 전통적 예절을 신랄하게 다룬 소설이다.『탁류』는 한국 서남 지역의 금강 유역에 모여 사는 하층민들, 그들의 삶을 탁류에 비유하여 실감나게 묘사하고 있다.

채만식의 후기 작품들은 좀 더 신랄하고 자기 성찰적이다.「민족의 죄인」(1948~49)은 일제 식민통치에 적극적

to set out in the world, as well as the class differences so distinct in Korean society past and present. In other stories from the 1920s and 1930s Ch'ae focuses more specifically on the plight of the unemployed young intellectuals turned out by the modernization movement in colonial Korea. The impecunious young intellectual making the rounds of publishing houses and pawnshops is portrayed with devastating accuracy in "A Ready-Made Life."

Two novels from the late 1930s are among his most important works. *Peace Under Heaven* (T'aep'yŏngch'ŏnha, 1938) is a pointed treatment of traditional Korean etiquette in the person of one who thrived materially but wasted spiritually during the Japanese occupation. *Muddy Waters* (T'angnyu 탁류, 1938-39) is a realistic portrait of the underclass populating the Kŭm River basin in southwestern Korea; their lives are compared to a muddy current.

Ch'ae's later works are more bitter and introspective. "An Enemy of the People" (Minjok ŭi choein 민족의 죄인, 1948-49) is a semiautobiographical apologia for those branded as collaborators for their failure to actively oppose Japanese colonial rule. In this and other stories, the author's wit is tempered not only by his struggle with lung disease but by the spiritu-

으로 반대하지 못했다는 이유로 반역자로 낙인찍힌 사람들을 위한 반자전적 변론이다. 이 작품은 물론, 그 외의 다른 작품들에서도 작가의 재치는 그 기세가 꺾이게 되는데, 그가 당시 폐질환으로 고생하고 있었다는 사실뿐 아니라, 식민지화된 사회에서의 예술가의 역할을 감당해야 하는 정신적 피로가 또 다른 이유일 것이다.

「맹순사」(1946),「미스터 방」,「논 이야기」(1946), 그리고 「처자」(1948, 같은 제목의 사후 발표작과는 다른 작품임)는 해방 후 한국사회에 대한 비관적인 스케치들이다.「처자」는 파벌로 인한 내분의 희생자들이 흔히 시골로 추방당하는 조선의 정치사를 반향시키고 있을 뿐 아니라, 현대사에 기록된 반대파들의 자택 감금까지도 이미 예견하고 있다. 이 이야기는 또한 여성에 대한 한국의 전통적 태도를 솔직하게 그리고 있다. 이 작품과 그 외의 작품들 속에서 채만식은 오랜 세월 억압되어온 한국 여인들에 대한 예리한 통찰력을 과시한다.

채만식은 소설 외에도 희곡, 영화 시나리오, 동화, 우화, 여행기, 그리고 수필 등을 발표했다. 그의 작품집은 창비 (서울)에서 1989년에 10권으로 집성되어 출간되었다.

al turmoil of having to come to grips with the role of the artist in a colonized society. "Constable Maeng" (Maeng sunsa 맹순사, 1946), "Mister Pang," "Once Upon a Paddy" (Non iyagi 논 이야기, 1946), and "The Wife and Children" (Ch'ŏja 처자, 1948; not to be confused with a posthumously published work of the same name) are pessimistic sketches of post-Liberation society. "The Wife and Children" echoes the political history of Chosŏn, in which victims of factional infighting were frequently banished to the countryside, as well as prefiguring contemporary history with its record of house arrests of dissidents. The story also offers an unvarnished view of traditional Korean attitudes toward women. In this and other works, Ch'ae offers keen insights into the long-standing oppression of Korean women.

In addition to his fiction Ch'ae published plays, screenplays, children's stories, fables, travel essays, and anecdotal essays (수필). His collected works were issued in ten volumes by the Ch'angjak kwa pip'yŏng sa publishing house in Seoul in 1989.

번역 및 감수 **브루스 풀턴, 주찬 풀턴**

Translated by Bruce and Ju-Chan Fulton

브루스 풀턴, 주찬 풀턴은 함께 한국문학 작품을 다수 영역해서 영미권에 소개하고 있다. 『별사-한국 여성 소설가 단편집』『순례자의 노래-한국 여성의 새로운 글쓰기』『유형의 땅』(공역, Marshall R. Pihl)을 번역하였다. 가장 최근 번역한 작품으로는 오정희의 소설집 『불의 강 외 단편소설 선집』, 조정래의 장편소설 『오 하느님』이 있다. 브루스 풀턴은 『레디메이드 인생』(공역, 김종운), 『현대 한국 소설 선집』(공편, 권영민), 『촛농 날개-악타 코리아나 한국 단편 선집』 외 다수의 작품의 번역과 편집을 담당했다. 브루스 풀턴은 서울대학교 국어국문학과에서 박사 학위를 받고 캐나다의 브리티시컬럼비아 대학 민영빈 한국문학 기금 교수로 재직하고 있다. 다수의 번역문학기금과 번역문학상 등을 수상한 바 있다.

Bruce and Ju-Chan Fulton are the translators of numerous volumes of modern Korean fiction, including the award-winning women's anthologies *Words of Farewell: Stories by Korean Women Writers* (Seal Press, 1989) and *Wayfarer: New Writing by Korean Women* (Women in Translation, 1997) and, with Marshall R. Pihl, *Land of Exile: Contemporary Korean Fiction*, rev. and exp. ed. (M.E. Sharpe, 2007). Their most recent translations are *River of Fire and Other Stories* by O Chŏnghŭi (Columbia University Press, 2012), and *How in Heaven's Name: A Novel of World War II* by Cho Chŏngnae (MerwinAsia, 2012). Bruce Fulton is co-translator (with Kim Chong-un) of *A Ready-Made Life: Early Masters of Modern Korean Fiction* (University of Hawai'i Press, 1998), co-editor (with Kwon Young-min) of *Modern Korean Fiction: An Anthology* (Columbia University Press, 2005), and editor of *Waxen Wings: The* Acta Koreana *Anthology of Short Fiction From Korea* (Koryo Press, 2011). The Fultons have received several awards and fellowships for their translations, including a National Endowment for the Arts Translation Fellowship, the first ever given for a translation from the Korean, and a residency at the Banff International Literary Translation Centre, the first ever awarded for translators from any Asian language. Bruce Fulton is the inaugural holder of the Young-Bin Min Chair in Korean Literature and Literary Translation, Department of Asian Studies, University of British Columbia.

바이링궐 에디션 한국 대표 소설 101

소망

2015년 1월 9일 초판 1쇄 발행

지은이 채만식 | **옮긴이** 브루스 풀턴, 주찬 풀턴 | **펴낸이** 김재범
기획위원 정은경, 전성태, 이경재 | **편집** 정수인, 이은혜, 김형욱, 윤단비 | **관리** 박신영
펴낸곳 (주)아시아 | **출판등록** 2006년 1월 27일 제406-2006-000004호
주소 서울특별시 동작구 서달로 161-1(흑석동 100-16)
전화 02.821.5055 | **팩스** 02.821.5057 | **홈페이지** www.bookasia.org
ISBN 979-11-5662-067-9 (set) | 979-11-5662-078-5 (04810)
값은 뒤표지에 있습니다.

Bi-lingual Edition Modern Korean Literature 101

Juvesenility

Written by Ch'ae Man-Sik | **Translated by** Bruce and Ju-Chan Fulton
Published by Asia Publishers | 161-1, Seodal-ro, Dongjak-gu, Seoul, Korea
Homepage Address www.bookasia.org | **Tel**. (822).821.5055 | **Fax**. (822).821.5057
First published in Korea by Asia Publishers 2015
ISBN 979-11-5662-067-9 (set) | 979-11-5662-078-5 (04810)

금기와 욕망 Taboo and Desire

바이링궐 에디션 한국 대표 소설 set 6

운명 Fate

미의 사제들 Aesthetic Priests

식민지의 벌거벗은 자들 The Naked in the Colony